TOASTY

Sarah Hwang

MARGARET FERGUSON BOOKS
HOLIDAY HOUSE · NEW YORK

To Mom, Dad, and my little brother, Jason,
for being my loving family and always encouraging
me to be the best I can be.

To my friend and agent, Shadra. I looked forward
to writing this dedication to you!
A million thank-yous for always believing in me.

Margaret Ferguson Books
Copyright © 2021 by Sarah Hwang
All Rights Reserved
HOLIDAY HOUSE is registered in the U.S. Patent and Trademark Office.
Printed and bound in January 2021 at Toppan Leefung, DongGuan, China.
The artwork was created with acrylic paint, color pencil, and digital collage.
www.holidayhouse.com
First Edition
1 3 5 7 9 10 8 6 4 2

Library of Congress Cataloging-in-Publication Data

Names: Hwang, Sarah, author, illustrator.
Title: Toasty / by Sarah Hwang.
Description: First edition. | New York : Holiday House, [2021]
Audience: Ages 4 to 6. | Audience: Grades K–1. | Summary: Toasty, a
piece of toast, believes he is a dog deep down in his crumbs, but realizes
he is very different from all the other dogs.
Identifiers: LCCN 2020016459 | ISBN 9780823447077 (hardcover)
Subjects: CYAC: Bread—Fiction. | Dogs—Fiction. | Identity—Fiction.
Classification: LCC PZ7.1.H915 To 2021 | DDC [E]—dc23
LC record available at https://lccn.loc.gov/2020016459

ISBN: 978-0-8234-4707-7 (hardcover)

This is Toasty.

Toasty loved watching the dogs outside his window play.

He loved how they barked and ran with each other in the park.

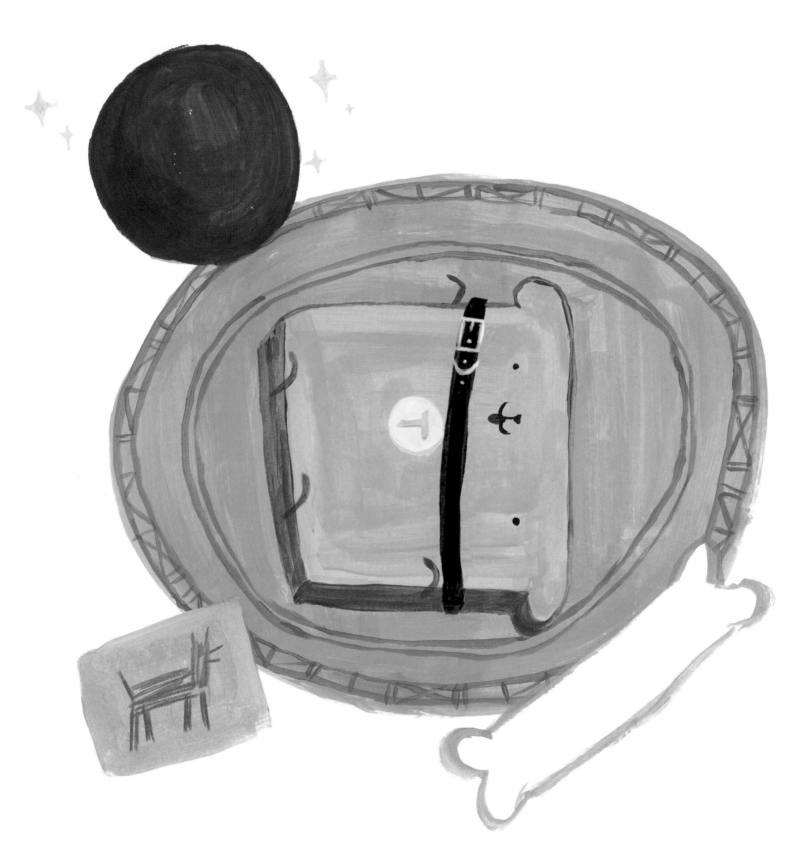

He loved them so much he wanted to be a dog.

Toasty knew there were some differences.
Most dogs have four legs.

But Toasty had two legs
and two arms.

Some dogs sleep in dog houses.
But Toasty slept in a toaster.

Dogs usually have hair or fur.
But Toasty had neither.

In fact, Toasty was

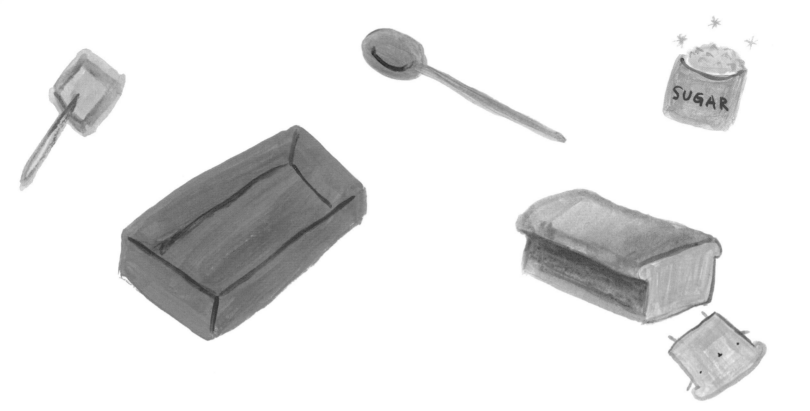

made of bread.

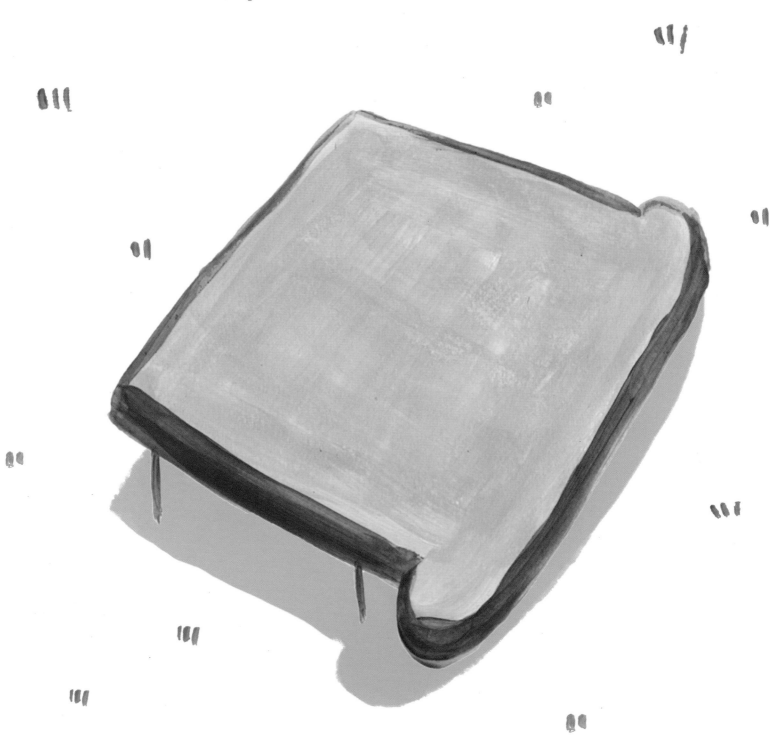

Toasty tried to run like a dog, but when he got on his two hands and two feet, all he was able to see was the ground.

Toasty chased a cat, but he was no match for it.

And when Toasty rolled in a puddle, he ended up soggy.

Surprisingly, Toasty *could* bark like a dog.

In spite of so many differences, Toasty decided to put on his best collar, grab his sparkly ball,

and go to the park to play with the dogs.

When Toasty found them, he tossed the ball high in the air.

But the dogs did not chase it.
They chased Toasty instead.
Uh-oh, this is not looking good for Toasty.

RUN TOASTY

RUN!!

He threw off his collar to distract them.

Just in time, Toasty spotted a sandwich nearby and jumped on top to hide.

The dogs came closer
and closer
and closer until suddenly . . .

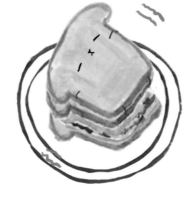

A girl grabbed her sandwich
and said, "Hey, that's mine!"

Then she sniffled and sneezed the biggest sneeze.

ACHOO!!

The girl sat down to take a bite and heard "WOOF! WOOF!"

She looked around to see who was barking and realized it was coming from her sandwich.

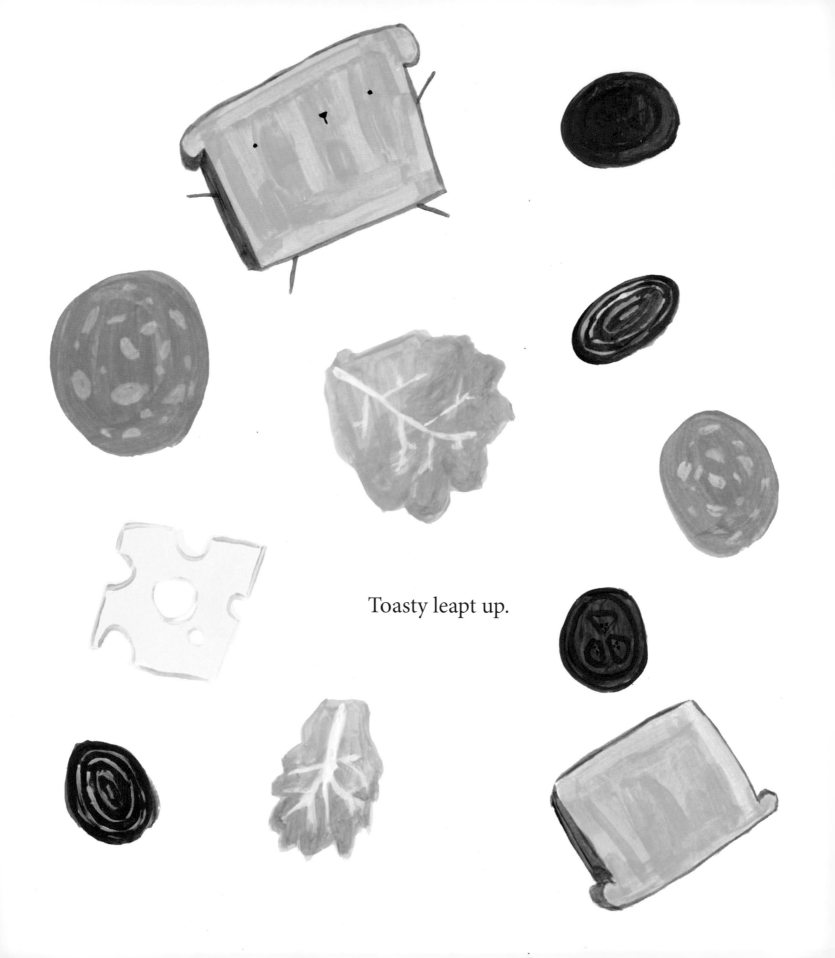

Toasty leapt up.

The girl laughed.

"I've always wanted a dog," she said, "but I'm allergic."

*WOOF. WOOF. WOOF.
WOOF. WOOF.

*Translation: Can I be your dog?

"You'd be the perfect dog for me."

Toasty and the girl played for the rest of the day.

PAW!!

And the day after that.

And the day after that.

They became the best of friends.

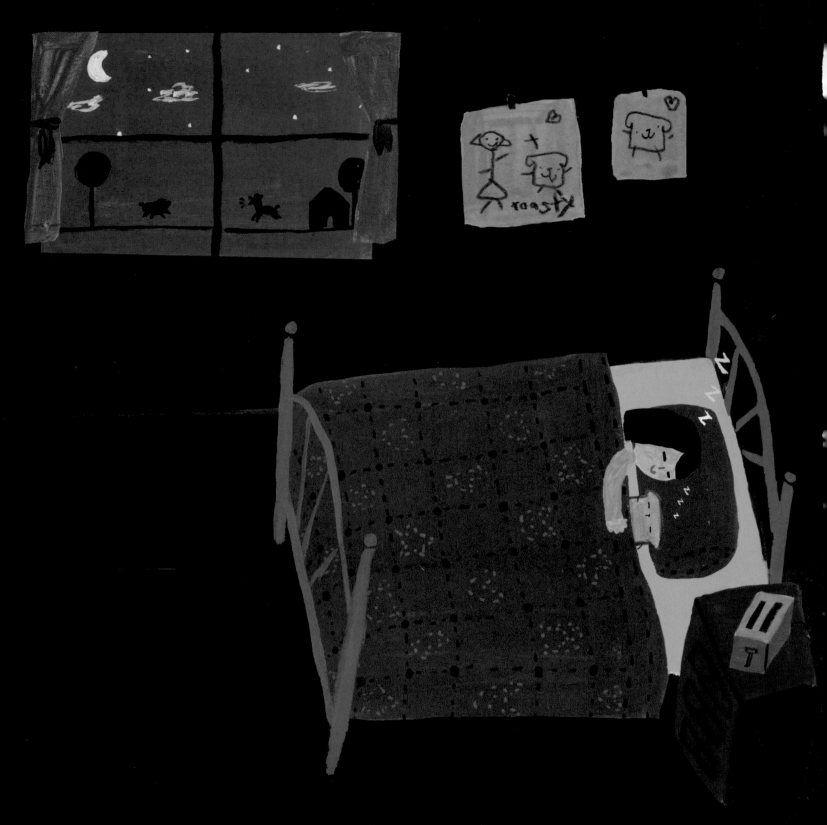

Toasty was different from the other dogs.
But the girl loved Toasty.
And Toasty loved her too.